For Sand Castles or Seashells

by Gail Hartman
illustrated by Ellen Weiss

BRADBURY PRESS/NEW YORK

Bradbury Press
An Affiliate of Macmillan, Inc.
866 Third Avenue, New York, NY 10022
Collier Macmillan Canada, Inc.

The text of this book is set in ITC Zapf International Light.
The illustrations are rendered in watercolor and colored pencil.

Printed and bound in Singapore
First American Edition
10 9 8 7 6 5 4 3 2 1

Library of Congress Cataloging-in-Publication Data
Hartman, Gail.
For sand castles or seashells/by Gail Hartman;
illustrated by Ellen Weiss.
p.   cm.
Summary: Depicts the alternative uses of such places as a tree
stump, busy street, and rain puddle.
ISBN 0-02-743091-X
[1. Play—Fiction.] I. Weiss, Ellen, ill. II. Title.
PZ7.H26733Fn 1990
[E]—dc20   89-35994 CIP AC

For Annie and Christine
—G.H.

To my niece, Maia
—E.W.

MY WINDOW

for keeping
out the rain

or letting in the sun

MY BACKYARD

for planting a garden

or playing hide-and-seek

A BUSY STREET

for riding in a bus

or marching in a parade

A SANDY BEACH

for building sand castles

or finding
seashells

A BIG HILL

for hiking up

or sledding down

A BLUE LAKE

for rowing a boat

or swimming
with Mom

A TREE STUMP

for picnicking on

or jumping off

A GRASSY FIELD

for looking at bugs

or watching clouds

A RAIN PUDDLE

for floating leaves

or stamping feet

A JUNGLE GYM

for climbing
right side up

or hanging
upside down

A FRONT DOOR

for going out

or coming home

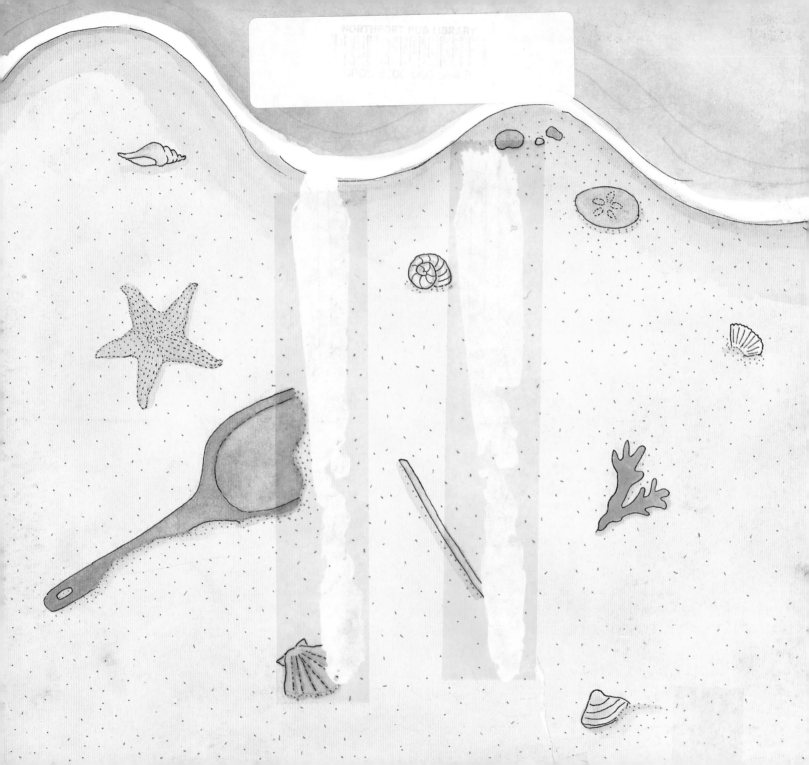